Disney

GRAVITY FALLS

ONCE UPON A SWINE

Adapted by Tracey West

Based on the series created by Alex Hirsch

Part One is based on the episode "The Time Traveller's Pig,"
written by Aury Wallington, Alex Hirsch

Part Two is based on the episode "Land Before Swine,"
written by Tim McKeon, Alex Hirsch

Disney XD

Disney PRESS

New York • Los Angeles

Printed in the United States of America
First Edition
10 9 8 7 6 5
FAC-025438-20079

Library of Congress Control Number: 2014936538
ISBN 978-1-4847-1140-8

For more Disney Press fun, visit www.disneybooks.com
Visit DisneyChannel.com

SUSTAINABLE
FORESTRY
INITIATIVE

Certified Chain of Custody
Promoting Sustainable Forestry

www.sfiprogram.org
SFI-01054

The SFI label applies to the text stock.

CHAPTER ONE

IT WAS A BEAUTIFUL day in Gravity Falls, and Stan Pines was in the middle of another moneymaking scheme. Workers were busily setting up rides, game booths, and food stands for the first ever Mystery Fair.

"There she is, Mabel!" he proudly told his great-niece, sweeping his arm to acknowledge the forest clearing. "The cheapest fair money can rent! I spared every expense."

"Aaaaaaaaaaaaaah!" *Whomp!*

Dipper, Mabel's twin brother, landed next to them in a blue ride cart.

"I think the sky tram is broken," he said. "Also, most of my bones."

Stan chuckled. "This guy. All right, all right, I got a job for you two. I printed up a bunch of fake safety inspection certificates. Go slap one on anything that looks like a lawsuit." He handed them each a stack of paper.

"Grunkle Stan, is that legal?" Mabel asked.

"When there's no cops around, anything's legal," he said. Then he marched over to Soos, the Mystery Shack's handyman. Soos was busy welding a metal arm onto the side of a tank of clear water.

"How's that dunk tank coming along?" Stan asked.

Soos lifted up his welding mask. "Almost ready to go, Mr. Pines."

Stan punched the target painted on the metal arm. Perfect! People could throw balls at it as hard as they wanted to, but that arm wasn't going to budge. He would be sitting high and dry on top of the dunk tank all day.

"Ha! There's nothing on Earth that could knock me down," Stan said.

"Yeah, except for, like, a futuristic laser arm cannon," Soos said.

Stan patted the pockets of his black suit. "Hey, you haven't seen my red screwdriver, have you? Darn thing went missing."

"Maybe some magical creature or paranormal thingum took it," Soos randomly suggested.

"You've been spending too much time with those kids!" Stan said.

Ever since Mabel and Dipper had come to visit him for the summer, they had been experiencing strange things in the woods of the Pacific Northwest—everything from monsters to a kid with spooky psychic powers. But Stan never seemed to believe them.

So he probably wouldn't have believed it if he knew the truth: a paranormal thingum *did* have Stan's screwdriver. He was a chubby, bald man in a gray suit. He ducked behind the nearby portable potties, hiding.

"The mission is proceeding as planned," he said into his wristwatch. "Over!"

Then he used the screwdriver

to adjust the watch. First, a camouflage pattern of trees appeared on his suit. Then a pattern of water. Finally, the suit turned the same mint-green color as the portable potties. With a grin, he walked away.

"It's twelve o'clock! The dunk tank is now open!" Stan called out from where he sat within the dunk tank, with his feet resting in the water. He had one goal today: to get as many suckers as possible to waste their money trying to dunk him. A crowd had already gathered around him.

"Who wants a piece of me?" he said to the onlookers.

The spectators threw dozens of balls at the target on the metal arm, but Stan didn't plunge into the water like he was supposed to. He laughed at them, and they didn't seem pleased. In fact, they seemed downright insulted. Stan's goal of not getting dunked—and making more money—was working.

Dipper had a goal, too: to get Wendy, the

fifteen-year-old who worked at the Mystery Shack, to have a perfect day with him at the fair.

And Mabel's goal was pretty much the same as always: to have fun!

Dipper was working on his goal at the Mystery Hot Dog stand, where he and Wendy got question-mark-shaped hot dogs on sticks.

"How do they get them into this shape?" Dipper said. "It's unnatural!"

Wendy held up her mustard-doused hot dog. She placed it at the end of the DELICIOUS sign hanging over the stand.

"But, Dipper, they're so . . . delicious?"

They both laughed, and then mustard dripped onto the sleeve of Wendy's plaid shirt.

"Oh, boo! I'll be right back," she said, and then she strolled away.

"I'll be right here!" Dipper called out. Then he chuckled and added weakly, "I love you."

Mabel walked up to Dipper, holding cotton candy in each hand. "Look at you two! Getting all romantic at the fair!"

"Isn't it amazing?!" Dipper asked. "I just dove in. I said, 'Hey, you wanna hang out at the fair?' And you know what she said?! 'Yeah, I guess so.' It totally worked! I took your advice about just going for it, and it's finally paying off."

"When are you going to learn, Dipper? I'm always right about everything," Mabel said. Then she sniffed the air. "Hey, do you smell a gallon of body spray?"

A tall teen with black hair hanging over his face walked up.

"Hey, either of you *dorks* seen Wendy around?" Robbie asked them.

"Who wants to know?" Dipper asked, even though he knew perfectly well who Robbie was—someone who'd most likely ruin his perfect day!

Robbie grabbed a piece of Mabel's cotton candy and popped it in his mouth.

"Hey!" Mabel yelled.

Robbie ignored her. He put his foot on an old crate and struck a pose. "Yeah, I got some new supertight jeans," he said. "Thought she might wanna check 'em out."

"Yeah, you know, I think I saw her in the bottomless pit," Dipper said. "You should really go jump in there."

"Maybe I will, smart guy," Robbie said sarcastically, and then strolled away, bumping into Dipper as he left.

"He is such a jerk!" Mabel said.

"Yeah, but he's a jerk with tight pants and a guitar," said Dipper. "I need to keep him away from Wendy at all costs."

Mabel put a hand on his shoulder. "Don't worry, brother. Whatever happens, I'll be right here, supporting you every step of the—"

Her eyes got wide, and she dropped her cotton candy. "Oh my gosh, a pig!" she squealed, pointing to a flier that read WIN A PIG.

Mabel followed the arrow on the flier to the Win a Pig booth, running as fast as she could. Inside, Farmer Sprott was standing in the mud with a bunch of pink baby pigs.

"If you can guess the critter's weight, you can take the critter home!" he announced.

Mabel leaned over the fence. She locked eyes with one of the pigs.

"Oink-el!"

"He said 'Mabel'!" Mabel shrieked. "Either that or 'doorbell.' Did you say 'Mabel' or 'doorbell'?"

"Oink-el!"

Mabel gasped. She was *sure* he had said her name. This was the pig of her dreams!

Then Pacifica Northwest and two of her friends walked past. Pacifica was super popular and had never been nice to Mabel.

"Oh, look, Mabel found her *real* twin," Pacifica said. Her posse snickered.

Mabel ignored them. She waved to Farmer Sprott. "Sir, I must have that pig!"

"Ah, yes, ol' Fifteen-Poundy. So how much are you guessing he weighs?" the farmer asked.

"Um, fifteen pounds?" Mabel said.

"Are you some kind of witch?" he asked. "Well, here's your pig."

The farmer handed him to Mabel, and she hugged the pig to her.

"Everything is different now," she whispered to the pig.

WHILE MABEL showered her pig with love, Dipper and his secret crush wandered around the fair. Wendy pointed to a game stand with prizes hanging overhead—some kind of weird-looking pink-and-purple stuffed animal.

"Whoa, check it out," Wendy said. "I don't

know if it's a duck or a panda, but I want one!"

Dipper studied the stand. To win the prize, you had to throw a ball at a pyramid of milk bottles and knock them down.

"My uncle taught me the secret to these games," Dipper said. "You aim for the carny's head, and take the prize when he's unconscious."

Wendy laughed. "Nice."

Dipper gave a ticket to the game attendant. "One ball, please."

"You only get one chance," the guy said flatly.

Dipper closed one eye, taking aim. "And-a-one! And-a-two! And-a—"

He threw the ball as hard as he could.

Whomp! It missed the bottles and bounced off the shelf behind them.

Bonk! The ball bounced back and hit Wendy right in the eye!

"Ow! My eye!" she cried.

Dipper panicked. "Oh my gosh! Oh my gosh! Wendy, are you okay?"

"Does it look swollen?" she asked as her eye turned purple-black and swelled to the size of an orange.

"Everything's gonna be fine," Dipper said. "Don't worry! I'll . . . I'll go get some ice!"

He rushed back to the Mystery Shack and grabbed a bag of ice. He raced through the crowd and . . . *bam!* He bumped into the strange bald man in the gray suit. The ice bag flew from Dipper's hands, spilling ice cubes all over the grass.

"Hey, watch where you're going, man!" Dipper said. He frantically scooped the ice back up—but he was too late.

Robbie was standing at the game booth, holding a cone of grape-flavored ice over Wendy's black eye.

"All right, just ease your eyeball into that Freezy-cone," he told her.

"Robbie, thanks. That's really sweet," she said. "The gesture *and* the flavored syrup."

"Yeah, I was just here in the right place at the right time," Robbie said. "You know, I've been meaning to ask you, we've been spending a lot of time together and I was wondering if maybe you wanted to go out with me?"

Dipper held his breath, terrified.

"Yeah, I guess so," Wendy said with a shrug.

Dipper gawked. This was his worst nightmare!

Mabel came running up. "Look, Dipper! I won my pet pig! His name is Waddles! I called him that because he waddles!" She wiggled her pig.

Dipper sighed. "Everything is different now," he said to no one specifically, gazing into space. His bag broke and all the ice cubes fell out of it.

"What are you looking at?" Mabel asked.

Dipper pointed at Robbie and Wendy. Robbie took Wendy's hand and they ran to the Tunnel of Love and Corn Dogs ride.

"Oh," Mabel said, understanding.

Dipper wandered off, and Mabel didn't find him again until hours later, after dark. Dipper was stretched out on Slopey Toss, one of the games, moaning and looking up at the stars.

Suddenly, Waddles appeared in front of him, dressed in doctors' scrubs.

"Paging Dr. Waddles! We got a boy here with a broken heart," Mabel teased, but Dipper didn't smile. "Come on, man! These are the jokes!"

"Mabel, do you ever wish you could go back and undo just one mistake?" Dipper asked.

"Nope! I do everything right all the time!" she replied confidently.

"I mean, Wendy only went out with Robbie because he was there with the ice, and she only needed ice because of the ball, and I would have had the ice if it wasn't for—" He sat up. "That guy!"

He pointed to the bald man in the gray suit, who was by the Ferris wheel fiddling with his watch.

"Hey, you—tool belt! You ruined my life!" Dipper yelled, stomping up to him.

The man looked surprised. "Huh?"

"Don't 'huh' me! I've seen you before! What's the deal? Are you following us?" Dipper asked.

"And why are you bald? What's that about?" Mabel asked him.

"My position has been compromised!" the stranger cried. "Assuming stealth mode!"

He started adjusting his watch, but the device malfunctioned. First he turned rainbow colors, then a pattern of a misty island, dinosaurs in sap, an arcade game, and then his suit turned back to gray.

"Color match. Initiating color match. Dang it!"

"That's *amazing*," Mabel said, and then she gasped. "Are you from the future or something?"

"Uh, no, who told you that?" the man asked, starting to perspire. Then he pushed something into Mabel's face. "Memory wipe!"

"This is a *baby* wipe," Mabel said, peeling it off.

He sighed and sat on a bale of hay. "All right. You've cornered me. I'm a time traveler."

"So wait a minute," Dipper said. "If you're from the future, do you have, like, a time machine or something?"

"That's kind of how it works," the bald man replied.

Dipper gazed up at Robbie and Wendy, who were riding the Ferris wheel together. An idea started to form.

"Could I borrow it?" he asked the time traveler.

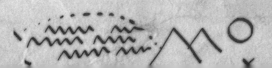

CHAPTER THREE

"**C**OME ON, can I use your time machine just once?" Dipper asked.

"Out of the question!" the strange man replied. He took an ordinary-looking tape measure off his tool belt. "You know, this is sensitive, extremely complicated time equipment."

"It looks like a tape measure," Dipper remarked.

The man was clearly insulted. "You shut your time-mouth!"

Dipper turned to his sister. "This making any sense to you?"

"I think he's just crazy!" Mabel whispered.

"Oh, you don't believe me?" the man asked. He pulled out the strip of the measuring tape.

Poof! He disappeared.

Poof! He reappeared, wearing clothes from Elizabethan England.

"Guess where I was?" he asked.

"Whoa!" cried Dipper and Mabel, impressed.

"That's right!" bragged the man. "Fifteen years ago there was a costume store right here! One second."

He pulled the tape measure again. *Poof!* He disappeared and then reappeared in his gray suit, which was in flames—a side effect of time travel. "Oh, heck! Pat down!" he cried, putting out the small fires on his sleeves. Then he placed the tape measure back in his tool belt.

"So, who are you again?" Mabel asked.

"Blendin Blandin," the time traveler replied. "Time Anomaly Removal Crew, Year Twenty Sñeventy Twelve. My mission is to stop a series of time anomalies that are supposed to happen at this very location. But I don't see any anomalies. I don't know if it's some kind of paradox or if I'm just really tired."

Dipper had an idea. "You know, you sound like you could use a break," he said.

Mabel nodded, catching on to Dipper's plan. "Definitely. Definitely. Might we recommend one of the various attractions at the Mystery Fair?" she asked, holding out some tickets.

"You know what? What the heck! I'm worth it!" Blendin cried, grabbing the tickets from her. "But I got my eye on you."

Dipper and Mabel followed him to the Rusty Barrel Rodeo ride, where one could climb into rusty barrels that spun around . . . and around . . . and around. Soos was working the ride.

"One, please," said Blendin, handing over his ticket.

"Aw, sorry, dude, but you're gonna have to take off your belt for the ride," Soos said. "One of your tools might fly off and accidentally fix something."

Blendin removed the belt and handed it to Soos. "Guard it with your life."

"I will watch it like a hawk, dude," Soos promised as Blendin hopped onto the ride. Then Soos put it on a barrel and turned his back on it.

Dipper saw his chance. He quickly grabbed the tape measure, and he and Mabel ran back to the Mystery Shack.

"Here it is, Mabel," he said, staring at it. "Our ticket to any moment in history!"

"Let's get two dodos and force them to make out!" Mabel suggested. She'd always felt bad that the birds had gone extinct.

"No! We gotta be smart about this!" Dipper

insisted. "All that paradox talk kind of freaked me out. All I'm going to do is go back and fix my one mistake. If I don't miss that ball throw, I won't hit Wendy in the eye, and Robbie won't comfort her, and they won't start going out."

"I'm coming, too!" Mabel said. "I wanna relive the greatest moment of my life—winning Waddles!" She kissed the pig on the cheek.

Dipper slowly pulled out the tape measure until he saw the perfect amount of time to go back: six hours. Then he stopped.

"See you later," he told Waddles.

"See you *earlier!*" Mabel said.

Dipper pressed a button on the tape measure. *Poof!*

The twins appeared right back in the Mystery Shack exactly six hours before. Dipper quickly patted down a small fire that broke out on his hat. Then he and Mabel raced for the door and stepped outside.

The sun was shining. Stan's voice rang out.

"It's twelve o'clock! The dunk tank is now open!"

Dipper looked at Mabel and grinned. "Do-over?"

"Do-over!" Mabel cried. She ran up to the pig stand.

"If you can guess the—" Farmer Sprott began.

"Fifteen pounds!" she yelled, grabbing Waddles. "And yes, I am a witch!"

Meanwhile, Dipper found Wendy over by the ball game.

"There you are," Wendy said. "Hey, what happened to your hat?"

"Nothing," Dipper said. He pointed to the stuffed animals. "Hey, what's that?"

"Whoa! Check it out," Wendy said. "I don't know if it's a duck or a panda, but I want one."

Dipper handed the attendant a ticket. "One ball, please."

"You only get one chance," the guy said.

"That's what you think. One panda-duck coming right up!" Then he lowered his voice. "Okay, Dipper, second chance. Don't mess this up."

He gripped the ball. This time, he aimed a little lower. He threw a little harder, and . . .

"Yes!" He knocked over the bottles. But the ball landed on the edge of a piece of wood and bounced back toward Wendy. . . .

"Ow! My eye!" Wendy wailed.

"What?" Dipper couldn't believe it. He had knocked down the bottles! This shouldn't have happened!

"Does it look swollen?" Wendy asked, and

then she suddenly smiled. "Oh, hey, Robbie!" she said.

Robbie strolled up, holding a Freezy-cone. "So, anyway, we've been hanging around each other a lot, and I've been wondering if, uh, you wanted to go out with me?"

Dipper stared at them, wide-eyed. He couldn't believe this was happening again.

"Yeah, I guess so," Wendy replied.

Robbie nodded. "Sweet!"

Dipper's eye twitched.

He ran to find Mabel. "The exact same thing happened twice!" he told her. "It was spooky!"

"Ooh, maybe it was a time curse!" Mabel said. "Waddles, can you say 'time curse'?"

"*Oink! Oink!*"

Mabel squealed and hugged him. "Your face is so fat!"

Dipper was thoughtful. "Is it possible that the forces of time naturally conspire to undo any new outcomes?" he wondered out loud. "No, no. I just need to try again. Third time's the charm."

"How hard can it be?" Mabel asked.

They were about to find out. . . .

CHAPTER FOUR

NO MATTER how many attempts it would take him, Dipper was determined to go back in time to set things right with Wendy. If all went according to plan, he'd win the prize for her, the ball wouldn't hit her eye, and he'd be totally cool in her (two good) eyes. No matter what, he just couldn't let Robbie ask her out. He and Mabel pulled the tape measure back.

Poof!

They landed right back at the hour of 12 noon. Mabel won Waddles again.

This time, Dipper threw the ball with his left hand instead of his right hand. It knocked over the bottles, hit a board, and ricocheted back at Wendy's face.

"Ow! My eye!" Wendy cried.

Robbie appeared immediately. "Hey, you all right?"

Dipper had failed again. He found Mabel taking pictures in a photo booth with Waddles, and they tried once more.

Poof!

Mabel won Waddles again.

This time, Dipper stood on Wendy's left side instead of her right side. He threw the ball, and this time it hit a stuffed animal, bounced off the attendant's nose, and then...

"Ow! My eye!" Wendy cried.

Along came Robbie again. "Oh, bad luck."
So Dipper tried again.
Poof!
Mabel won Waddles. They shared a slice of pizza.

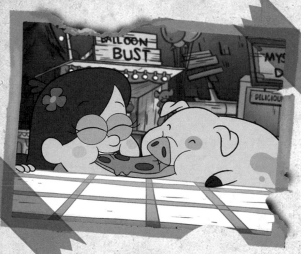

Dipper tried to get out of throwing the ball altogether.

"So, Wendy, how badly do you really want that stuffed animal thing?" he asked.

"More than anything in the world, Dipper," she replied.

Dipper sighed. "Okay."

This time, he threw the ball low. It hit the wooden stand holding the bottles. It bounced and hit the bag of balls hanging from the roof. The bag broke, and ball after ball bombarded Wendy's face.

"Ow!" Wendy cried as Robbie appeared again.

"I love my pig!" Mabel announced to the world as she sat next to Waddles on the Ferris wheel.

Poof!

Dipper knew there had to be a strategy. He started doing quick calculations on the glass of the popcorn machine.

"If I adjust the ball for wind speed, factoring cotton candy . . ."

"Face it, Dipper, you're obviously fated to have a bad day at the fair," Mabel told him as she knitted a sweater for her pig.

"Just like I'm fated to be with Waddles!"

"There's just one variable missing," Dipper said thoughtfully.

"What's a variable?" Mabel asked.

Dipper stared at his calculations. Then his eyes lit up. "Ha! That's it! I figured out a way to win the toss, not hit Wendy, and stop Wendy and Robbie from going out."

"Awesome! I'm gonna go win my pig again!" Mabel said.

"Whoa, whoa, whoa!" Dipper said, grabbing her arm. "You can't leave. I need you for my plan."

"But what about Waddles?" Mabel asked.

"It'll just take a few minutes. You can win Waddles afterward," Dipper said. "Let's go!"

Dipper dragged her away. Soon he was back at the game stand with Wendy. He handed in his ticket and got his ball. Then he stuck his finger in his mouth and held it up to test the wind direction.

Perfect! He was ready.

"And-a-one, and-a-two, and-a . . ."

He threw the ball—not at the bottles, but at the top of a nearby tent. The ball rolled down the top of the tent, whose roof curved up, and it sailed to the roof of the Mystery Shack, where Mabel was waiting. The ball landed in the gutter and she tilted up the end of the gutter just in time.

The ball flew to the target on Stan's dunk tank. It hit the target and bounced off without dunking Grunkle Stan. Then it knocked a slice of pizza out of one guy's hands, knocked the Freezy-cone out of Robbie's hands, and crashed into the bottles.

Thunk! The bottles went down. The ball fell safely to the floor.

Wendy was fine!

The attendant held out her prize. "Your stuffed creature of indeterminate species, miss."

"Oh, awesome!" Wendy cried.

Then Robbie walked up. "So, I was wondering if, uh, you, uh . . ."

"Look what Dipper got for me!" Wendy interrupted him, holding out the animal.

Robbie shrugged. "Pssh. Whatever. Can't even tell what species it is. Stupid." He pulled his hood over his head and shuffled away.

"What's his deal?" Wendy said. "Pssh. Looks like I came to the fair with the right guy!"

Dipper grinned from ear to ear.

Mabel watched Dipper and Wendy.

Dipper looked over toward her and gave her a thumbs-up.

"Anytime, Brosef," she said, smiling and returning the gesture. "Now to win my pig."

But as she approached Farmer Sprott's stand, she gasped. Pacifica had gotten there before her! And Farmer Sprott was handing over Waddles!

"It's all yours!" he told Pacifica. "No one else's! Ol' Fifteen-Poundy! Yours! Forever!"

Mabel screamed and ran to find Dipper. He was climbing out of the Tunnel of Love and Corn Dogs as Wendy ran ahead to get funnel cakes for them.

"Aaaaaaaaaaaaaaaaaaaaaaaaaaaaaaaaaaah!" Mabel screamed.

"What's wrong?" Dipper asked.

"Aaaaaaaaaaaaaaaaaaaaaaaaaaaaaaaaaaaaaaa-aaaaaaaaaaaaaaaaah!"

"I'll just wait until you're done," Dipper said.

Mabel stopped. "I'm done."

"Okay, what's wrong?" her brother asked.

"We messed up the time line!" Mabel said. "Pacifica saw the flier and won Waddles before I did! She took Waddles, Dipper!"

"Oh, Mabel, I'm sorry," Dipper said.

Mabel sighed. "It's okay. We just need to go

back and do things differently." She took the tape measure from him.

Dipper gasped and took it back. "Mabel, wait! Look, I did the math. In any other time line, Wendy ends up going out with Robbie! I can't mess up this day again!"

"But if we don't go back, then I'll lose Waddles forever!" Mabel cried, angrily reaching for the tape measure. She and Dipper tussled back and forth, trying to gain control of the tiny time machine.

"Give it back!" Dipper grunted.

He yanked hard, and the tape measure flew out of their hands. Dipper and Mabel grabbed the end of the tape. The carriage of the tape measure landed on the seat of one of the Tunnel of Love and Corn Dogs carts. When it started moving, it pulled the tape out farther, and farther, and then . . .

Poof!

Dipper and Mabel landed in the middle of a dirt road surrounded by tall pines. It looked like they were in Gravity Falls, except there was no fair, no Mystery Shack—and no people.

"*When* are we?" Dipper asked.

"The real question is, *when* are we?" Mabel said. "Oh, wait, did you already say that? 'Cause—"

"Yeah, I know," Dipper said.

Suddenly, the ground underneath their feet vibrated. A loud, rumbling sound filled the air.

"Do you hear that?" Dipper asked, and the twins turned around.

A herd of bison came stampeding down the road!

CHAPTER FIVE

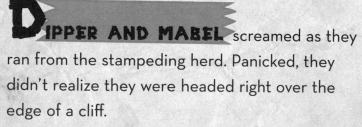

DIPPER AND MABEL screamed as they
ran from the stampeding herd. Panicked, they
didn't realize they were headed right over the
edge of a cliff.

"Aaaaaaaaaaaaaah!"

They plummeted down, but luck was on their

side. A covered wagon was passing by on the mountain trail just below. They crashed through the fabric cover and landed safely inside.

Outside, the trail guide rode a horse, leading the way.

"Be on the lookout for mountain lions, travelers!" he called out.

The grizzled camp cook walked alongside the wagon and held up a canteen. "Dysentery? Who wants dysentery?"

The wagon driver pulled at the reins. "Forge ahead, mighty oxen! For a new life awaits us on this Oregon Trail!"

"Where are we? The seventies?" Mabel asked Dipper.

"You sent us back a hundred and fifty years, genius!" her brother told her. "It's pioneer times!"

The wagon driver looked back and saw Dipper and Mabel. "By Trembley!" he exclaimed. "Fertilla, it seems you've given birth to two more children!"

Dipper and Mabel followed his gaze inside

the wagon, where five children surrounded their pioneer mother.

"It appears I have!" said the woman, Fertilla. "More little hands to render the tallow."

"Tallow? What?" Mabel asked.

A boy pointed at Mabel. "Her mouth is filled with silver, mother!"

"These are called braces," Mabel explained.

"Mabel, we can't start messing with the past!" Dipper hissed.

"Oh, says the guy who messed with the past all day and cost me my pig?" Mabel asked. "I'll mess with whatever I want!"

She took a calculator from her pocket. "Check it out! A magic button machine!"

Dipper grabbed the calculator from her. Mabel tapped her light-up pink sneakers on the floor of the wagon. "Shoes that blink!"

The pioneer family oohed.

Mabel pointed to the mom. "Hey, sister, who gets to vote in the future? Ladies! Up top!"

She held up her palm, and the mom instinctively slapped it.

"That's called a high five. Teach it to your friends."

Dipper grabbed the tape measure from her.

"Give me that! I'm gonna set the time line right!" he yelled. He quickly pulled out the tape.

"Hey! No!" Mabel lunged at him and took the tape measure just as they both . . .

Poof!

. . . found themselves in the shadow of an angry *T. rex.*

"Aaaaaaaaaaaaah!"

Mabel quickly pulled the tape measure.

Poof!

This time they landed far in the future. Buildings crumbled all around them as space-age cops ran past them, screaming, "It's coming!"

A giant baby floated toward them, shooting red lasers from its eyes.

"This future seems neat," Mabel remarked.

Dipper grabbed the tape measure from her. *Poof!*

They were back in Gravity Falls, but it wasn't the day of the fair. They were at Lake Gravity Falls, where Old Man McGucket was yelling about the Gobblewonker. Mabel snatched the tape measure back from Dipper. *Poof!* Now they were running past Grunkle Stan unveiling a wax statue of himself. *Poof!* And now they were running past the Mystery Shack, where they saw the Gnome Monster that had attacked them when they first came to Gravity Falls. These were all things that had happened to them already this summer.

The tape measure began to glow white-hot. It started to float out of Mabel's hands. Around them, snow piled up against the Mystery Shack.

"What did you do?!" Dipper asked as they skidded to a stop in the snow.

"I don't know!" Mabel wailed.

Then the white-hot light grew brighter and brighter. . . .

Poof!

46

They appeared in total darkness.

"It's nothing but inky blackness for miles," Dipper said, his voice rising in panic. "Mabel, don't you see? We've transported to the end of time!"

"Aaaaaaaaaaaaah!" they screamed.

"Wait, why does it smell so bad at the end of time?" Mabel asked.

Dipper discovered a door—and it opened. They were inside a portable potty!

"Look, we're back in the present!" Mabel exclaimed once they stepped outside.

"But which present?" Dipper asked.

Then he spotted Wendy holding her stuffed whatever-it-was—with no black eye.

"Yes!" Dipper cheered.

Then Pacifica walked by, dragging a reluctant Waddles on a leash.

"No!" Mabel yelled. She tried to grab the tape measure from Dipper. "Give me that thing! Dipper, give it back!"

She chased him around the potty, and he had to jump on top of it to escape her.

"Look, Mabel, it's over, okay," he called down. "Give it up! I've worked too hard to lose this."

"But what about Waddles? He was my soul mate," Mabel said sadly.

"You said that about a ball of yarn once," Dipper countered. "Do you really want Wendy to date Robbie?"

Mabel sighed. "I don't know." She took out the photo booth picture of her with Waddles, and tears formed in her eyes. She walked to a nearby totem pole and leaned her head against it.

"You're not guilt-tripping me, Mabel," Dipper said. "Not this time."

Mabel just banged her head against the totem pole. Again . . . and again . . . and again.

"Come on, Mabel,

I know you. You're gonna forget about this in a day. Here, hey, I'll prove it."

Poof!

He went ahead one day, and she was still banging her head against the totem pole.

Poof!

One week later, and she was still at it.

Poof!

One month later, and she hadn't stopped. Vines were snaking up her legs, and a snail had made a home on her shoulder.

"Waddles ... Waddles ..." she said weakly to herself.

Soos walked by, leading a tour group. "And if you look to your left, you'll see Miserable Mabel, the girl who went bonkers after her dreams were shattered by some heartless jerk. Oh, hey, Dipper."

Dipper groaned. He hated to see his sister like this. Almost more than he hated seeing Wendy going out with Robbie. With a sigh, he pulled the tape measure one last time.

Poof!

He was back at the fair, standing in front of the game stand with Wendy.

"I don't know if it's a duck or a panda, but I want one," Wendy said.

"Wendy, I just wanted to say that, well, people make mistakes, and when they do, you should forgive them," he told her. "And also that tight pants are overrated."

"Dude, you lost me," Wendy said.

"I know," Dipper said. He was about to lose her for real—maybe for good. He handed the ticket to the attendant.

"One ball, please."

CHAPTER SIX

"**OW! MY EYE!**" Wendy cried as the ball gave her a black eye.

Robbie appeared, right on schedule. "Hey, Wendy? Are you okay? You know, this is the perfect time for me to, uh, ask you something."

Dipper frowned. "It is done."

Mabel came running up with Waddles. She knocked Dipper down and Waddles licked his cheek.

"Dipper! Thank you! Thank you! Thank you!" cried Mabel happily, giving him a giant hug.

"*Oink!*" said Waddles.

Mabel grinned proudly. "He's saying 'thank you' in Pig. Aren't you, Waddles?"

"*Oink!*" Waddles replied.

Dipper looked at his sister. "I couldn't break your heart, Mabel. Besides, there's no way Wendy can date Robbie all summer, right?"

Suddenly, Dipper felt somebody snatch the

tape measure from his hand. It was Blendin, and he was angry.

"You two!" he yelled, pointing. "Do you have any idea how many rules you just broke? I'm asking. I wasn't there with you. It was probably a lot, right?"

Poof!

Two huge, muscled, futuristic-looking cops appeared out of nowhere. They wore black armored uniforms, each marked with a glowing green symbol of an hourglass. Each one had a name tag: Lolph and Dungren.

"Blendin Blandin?"

"Ah! The Time Paradox Avoidance Enforcement Squadron!" Blendin cried.

"That's right. And our phones have been ringing

off the hook. There's settlers high-fiving in the eighteen hundreds. And calculators littered through eight centuries!" said Lolph.

"You are under arrest for violations of the Time Travelers' Code of Conduct," Dungren informed him in a deep voice.

"It—it was those kids! And their leader, Waddles!" Blendin cried.

"That's a pig, Blendin," Dungren said, and the two time cops grabbed him by the arms and dragged him away.

"I'll—I'll get you for this," Blendin stuttered, pointing at Dipper and Mabel. "I'll go back in time and make sure your parents never meet!"

Dipper and Mabel looked themselves over.

"Well, we're still here," Dipper said.

"Guess he forgot to go back," said Mabel.

Then Stan's voice rang out through a megaphone.

"Ha! You suckers! Your pockets are empty and I'm still sitting high and dry!" he taunted from his perch inside the dunk tank.

The crowd loudly booed him.

"Yeah. 'Boo. Boo.' I love it!" he said. He scanned the crowd for more suckers just as Lolph and Dungren were walking by with Blendin.

"Hey, biceps!" he yelled, pointing at Lolph. "I'm talking to you, haircut. Take your best shot."

Without a word, Lolph raised his futuristic laser arm cannon.

Bam! The laser blast decimated the arm of the dunk tank. Stan's platform tipped over, and he splashed into the tank of icy cold water.

The crowd clapped and cheered.

Then . . . *poof!* The time cops and Blendin disappeared.

"So, I guess we never found out who was causing those time anomalies Blendin was looking for," Mabel said to Dipper.

Dipper froze. "Mabel, I think it was us!"

Mabel groaned. "My brain hurts."

Then Dipper spotted Wendy and Robbie. Robbie was handing Wendy a caramel apple.

Dipper sighed. "Aw, jeez, I've gotta deal with this all summer."

Mabel grinned at Dipper. "I'm on it."

She put down Waddles. The pig got a whiff of the caramel apple and charged toward Robbie.

Terrified, the teen dropped the apple and bolted. He crashed into a table, knocking over a pot of hot water that drenched his legs.

"My pants! They're shrinking!" Robbie wailed.

Everybody started laughing—even Wendy.

"Oh, man," Wendy said, winking at Dipper.

Dipper smiled and patted Waddles on the head. "That'll do, pig. That'll do."

CHAPTER ONE

IT WAS A night like any other in Gravity Falls. Sheriff Blubs and Deputy Durland sat in their squad car by the side of the road, watching for speeders. Durland intently scribbled something on a pad of paper.

"Focus, Deputy," Blubs said. "Easy ... easy ... careful there ... you almost got it."

Durland made one more line with his pencil ... which led right to the mouth of the shark in CAP'N BRAIN-TEASER'S FUN MAZE!

"Dang it! I almost got the treasure!" he complained.

"The time we spend together is treasure enough," the sheriff said.

Suddenly, the whole squad car began to shake, interrupting their tender moment.

"Hey, you feel that?" Sheriff Blubs asked.

With a sickening crunch of metal, something peeled off the top of the police car. The two officers stared at the sky as the roof of their car seemed to fly off on its own.

"Reckon we should report that," drawled Deputy Durland.

But Sheriff Blubs just grinned. "Or go for a ride in our new convertible!"

"Yee-hoooo!" cheered the deputy as they peeled off into the night.

If they had looked up at the full moon, they would have seen a mysterious winged creature soaring across the night sky . . . searching.

It was a morning like any other morning at the Mystery Shack. Stan was giving a tour to another bunch of gullible tourists. He drove a golf cart, pulling the tourists behind him in a tram.

"And if you look to your left, you'll see the world-famous Outhouse of Mystery!" he announced, pointing to the run-down outdoor toilet.

"Can I go to the bathroom?" a kid asked.

"Save all questions until after the tour!" Stan said.

Inside the Mystery Shack, Mabel watched Stan

drive the tourists into the woods. Mabel turned to Waddles and smiled.

"Finally, Waddles! We have the whole place to ourselves," Mabel said happily. "What do you think? Dance party?"

"*Oink!*" replied Waddles.

Mabel flipped the OPEN sign to CLOSED on the front door and turned up the music.

"Let the dance party begin!"

Mabel and Waddles danced. They boogied. They skipped and shimmied and swayed. They ate as many grape popsicles as they could. They put on silly sunglasses and took selfies.

"Yes! Yes! Yes!" Mabel cheered. Then she collapsed on the floor, exhausted. Waddles licked her hand, and Mabel sat up.

"Uh-oh! Cuddle time!" she said, and Waddles climbed into her lap. Mabel hugged him.

"Waddles, can I tell you a secret?" she asked. "You're my favorite pig in the whole world."

Then they closed their eyes for a nap. Stan walked in, humming and counting his money, and tripped over them.

"What are you doing on the floor?" he asked.

Mabel smiled. "Being cute and great."

Stan shook his head. "And I thought your brother was weird."

Mabel jumped up and put on a hat with a pine tree design on it, just like the one Dipper wore. "Uh, I'm Dipper," she said in a dumb guy voice. "I kiss a pillow with Wendy's face drawn on it! Ohhh, Wendy!"

Stan chuckled. "Ha! That's pretty good."

While he was talking, Waddles decided to snack on the bottom of Stan's trousers. Stan noticed and kicked him off.

"Outside! Now!" he growled.

Mabel clutched Waddles protectively. "No! Grunkle Stan! It's not safe for Waddles outside. There are predators! And barbecuers!"

Stan shrugged. "That's just the natural order. It's not my fault that he's potentially delicious."

"Waddles should be inside, like a person!" Mabel protested.

"People don't roll around in their own filth," Stan pointed out. "Except for Soos."

"And we're the lesser for it," Mabel said. "Maybe we're the ones who should be put outside. Huh? Huh? Think about it."

With one last glance at Stan, Mabel walked off.

Deep in the woods of Gravity Falls, Dipper and Soos were much happier than Mabel. Soos pulled his pickup truck in front of a big redwood tree. They both got out of the cab and sat in the open truck bed.

"Today's the day, Soos! Thanks for coming along on this mission," Dipper said.

"Dude, it's an honor. Today I'm sweating from heat *and* excitement," the big handyman said, wiping his forehead with his hand.

Dipper opened up a file folder and looked through the evidence he had gathered.

COP CAR CRUNCH

SHEEP SNATCHED

A MINOR PROBLEM

FOOTPRINT

"There's a monster out there!" he said. "In between the cop car top being ripped off and Farmer Sprott's sheep being taken, the whole town is talking! If we catch this thing, we'll be heroes!"

"Yeah, we'll get all the babes," Soos said. "You'll be fending off smooches with a stick!"

Dipper nudged him. "Ha, ha! Shut up, man!"

Soos nudged him back. "With a stick, dude."

Dipper hopped down from the bed. "Let's get this set up."

They worked together to rig up their plan. To do that, they needed to tie three different cameras to three trees. They strung up two of the cameras. The network of ropes holding them up created a complex web of strings back and forth between the trees, with a piece of steak on a stump in the center. Soos attached the last camera and then shinnied down the trunk to meet up with Dipper, who was sitting on a branch below. On the way back down, Soos's hands got stuck in sticky tree sap.

Dipper proudly looked at their handiwork.

"If everything goes according to plan, the creature will grab that steak, cross through the string, and set off cameras A, B, and C," he said.

"And nothing can go wrong," Soos said confidently. "High five!"

He slapped Dipper's hands, and their hands got stuck together.

"This was poorly planned," Dipper remarked.

Then . . . *whoosh!* Something flew by them at top speed, breaking through the ropes. All three cameras clicked on at once.

Dipper turned to Soos, thrilled. "We got it!"

CHAPTER TWO

IT WORKS FOR PI||||||||||||
||||||||||||||||||
||||||||||||||||||
|||||||||GS!!!!

BACK IN THE Mystery Shack, Mabel and Waddles were watching TV as Mabel knitted a sweater for Waddles. She had already knitted a red one for herself with a picture of Waddles on it. Waddles's sweater, of course, had a picture of Mabel on it.

Then a commercial came on the screen.

"Sick of constantly dropping your baby?" the announcer asked. "Then what you need is the Huggy Wuvvy Tummy Bundle!"

A picture of a baby-carrying backpack appeared on the screen.

"I know what you're thinking: does it work for pigs?" the announcer asked. "Yes, it works for pigs. Feel your pig's heartbeat next to yours. IT WORKS FOR PIIIIIIIIIIIIIIIIIIIIIIIIIIIIIIIIIIIGS!!!!"

Mabel's eyes widened. This was exactly what she needed!

"Grunkle Stan! I'm off to get a Huggy Wuvvy Tummy Bundle!" she cried, running into Stan's room. Her great-uncle was smoothing out his black suit and looking in the mirror.

"Isn't knitting matching sweaters enough?" Stan asked.

"Nope! Anyway, I need you to look after this little gentleman while I'm gone." She held out Waddles.

"Look, kid, I got a tour coming through in five minutes. I'm busy," Stan said.

"Grunkle Stan, I know you're not crazy about Waddles," Mabel said.

"He's a fat naked jerk," Stan said, straightening his tie.

"But you DO care about me," Mabel reminded him. "Promise me you won't let him outside."

Mabel looked up at Stan with the sweetest expression she could muster.

"Fine," he muttered. "Yeah, yeah, I promise."

"Thanks, Grunkle Stan!" Mabel said happily. She put down Waddles and scampered off to the store.

Stan leaned down and glared at Waddles.

"I'm watching you, pig," he warned, pointing a finger at him.

Waddles lifted up his hoof and gently touched Stan's finger. It was adorable, but Stan was immune to the pig's charms. He marched outside to meet his tour group. After they paid (Stan's favorite part of the tour), he led them around the main showroom of the Mystery Shack.

The showroom held a variety of strange and unusual objects: a deer's head with bat wings growing out of the neck; a giant dinosaur skull; and the World's Largest Donut (maybe), to name a few. Stan always said they looked real enough to fool the dumb tourists and looked cruddy enough to charm the smart ones.

There was one gag his tourists always loved. Stan walked up to a tall object covered by a sheet.

"And here are the most hideous creatures known to man!" he cried, pulling off the sheet with a flourish—to reveal a dusty mirror underneath.

The family of tourists saw their own reflections and giggled. Stan had them right in the palm of his hand.

"Right? Right? We have fun here," Stan said. He moved them all on to another item covered with a sheet. "But seriously, folks. *This* is something. I present to you, a unicorn made out of corn. The Corn-icorn!"

He pulled off the sheet—to reveal a wire frame of the Corn-icorn. All the corn was gone!

"What the—?" Then Stan noticed Waddles in the corner, curled up in the sweater Mabel made for him—and covered with bits of corn.

"What a rip-off!" said the tourist dad. "Kids, put down all the expensive souvenirs we were going to get you. We're leaving!"

The kids dropped the armfuls of souvenirs they were holding as their parents quickly shuffled them out of the Mystery Shack.

"Noooooooo!" Stan wailed, chasing them outside.

Dipper and Soos passed by him. Dipper's arms were filled with the cameras they had used in the woods.

"We did it!" Dipper said, entering the Mystery Shack. "It tripped the wire! Somewhere in these cameras is a photo of the creature!"

"Yes! Yes! I'm feeling such a rush right now!" Soos said, karate-chopping the air.

"I'm going to develop the film," Dipper said, bounding up the stairs to his room in the attic.

"I'll go make victory nachos!" offered Soos as he headed to the snack bar. "Dipper and Soos forever!"

Dipper quickly got to work, transforming his bedroom into a photographer's darkroom. He had used old-school cameras in the woods, and he needed chemicals—and almost complete darkness—to turn the film into prints.

He developed the first roll of film, hanging the photos on a clothesline to dry. Most of them just showed trees and branches, but what was that?

"That's a wing!" Dipper realized. "If camera B

got the wing, then the one that should have got the rest is camera C!"

He hurried to the tray of chemicals that held one of the photos from camera C. The image was just starting to form. As it got clearer and clearer, he could see a huge object. It had wings, but it was much bigger than a bird. What was it? Just a few more seconds . . .

"Who wants victory nachos?!" Soos yelled, throwing open the door.

Light flooded in, halting the chemical process. The image on the paper turned solid black. It was ruined!

"Noooooooooo!" Dipper cried.

Downstairs, Stan went outside holding Waddles under one arm. Making sure the coast was clear, he tied Waddles to a post and then hammered it into the ground.

"Just ten minutes without this pig in the house. Is that too much to ask? No," he said. He looked at Waddles in his red sweater. It was still tied to the ball of red yarn. "If Mabel asks, this never happened. Keep it quiet, pal."

Stan tucked a five-dollar bill into the rope around Waddles's neck and headed inside.

"But, Grunkle Stan, it's not safe out there! There's predators," he muttered, mimicking Mabel. "Oh, brother."

Suddenly, a huge wind brushed past Stan, knocking off his fez. Looking up, he saw a giant pterodactyl! It swooped down from the sky and snatched up Waddles in its talons.

Upstairs, Dipper was pretty ticked off at Soos. "No offense, Soos, but you have to take this stuff more seriously," he was saying. "I mean, what are the odds we'll ever get another picture of the—"

Screeeeeeeeeeeech!

The sound of the pterodactyl jolted them both. They ran to the window just in time to see the pterodactyl fly past. Frantic, they ran outside.

Stan was staring at the sky, shell-shocked.

"We haven't been hunting a monster—that thing was a dinosaur! Ha! They're not extinct!" said Soos.

Dipper was dumbfounded. "How is it possible a dinosaur survived for sixty-five million years?"

Soos nudged Stan. "Did you see it, Mr. Pines?"

"It—it took him," Stan said, gawking.

"Took what?" Dipper asked.

"The pig," Stan said. "It took Waddles."

"What did you say about Waddles?"

Stan turned around, horrified, to see Mabel riding up on her bike.

CHAPTER THREE

"**WHAT'S GOING ON?**" Mabel asked. "Why are you standing around all awkwardly?" She looked right and left. "And where's Waddles?"

Stan grabbed the post he had used to tie up Waddles and hid it behind his back.

"Uh, the good news is, you're getting a puppy!" he said.

Mabel narrowed her eyes suspiciously. "What happened?"

Stan couldn't bring himself to say it. "Well . . . see . . . the, um . . ."

Soos broke the news. "Dude, your pig sorta got eaten by a puh-terodactyl, bro."

"*What?*" Mabel asked in disbelief. She ran around in a panic, looking for her pig. "Waddles? Waddles?"

Her breathing got short and fast. "Where did he go? How did this happen?" she asked. "Grunkle Stan, you didn't put him outside?"

Dipper and Soos turned to look at Stan.

"What? Uh, no! I didn't put him anywhere. I'm not acting suspicious! *You're* acting suspicious. What's a pig?" Stan stammered. He had to think quickly.

"Uh, look, it went down like this, see?" he began. "So there I was, in the living room. I had him in my arms, feeding him one of those baby . . . food . . . tubes. Bottle or whatever. When all of a sudden, KA-BLAMMOS!"

"The puh-terodactyl?" Soos asked.

Stan nodded. "It crashed through the door and grabbed him right out of my hands! So I jumped on top of that sucker and punched his face as hard as I could. But he played dirty. He poked me right in the eye and I fell off his back. Then he flew off with your pig."

"Waddles!" Mabel wailed.

"'Why, why couldn't it have been me?' I yelled to the heavens," Stan told Mabel. He buried his face in his hands. Would the girl buy it?

Mabel threw her arms around him. "Oh, Grunkle Stan! You tried to save him!"

"Um, yep," Stan said, wincing slightly. "I'm a great man all right."

Dipper was skeptical. "You punched a pterodactyl in the face? I thought you didn't even believe in the supernatural."

"Dinosaurs aren't magic. They're just big lizards. Get off my back!" Stan snapped.

Tears formed in Mabel's eyes. "Oh, Waddles."

"That's it!" Dipper said angrily. "I wanted to catch that pterodactyl before . . . but now we *have* to. For Mabel, guys."

Soos piped in. "For Mabel! But how are we gonna find the little dude?"

Mabel looked around. There had to be some clue. . . .

And then she saw it—the red ball of yarn that was still attached to Waddles's sweater. The yarn had unraveled as the pterodactyl flew off with Waddles, and it led into the forest.

"Genius!" cried Dipper.

"Or you know, maybe we could just call it a day and hit the pool hall," Stan said, but everybody glared at him.

"Yeah!" he said weakly. "Let's go save Waggles!"

"Waddles," Mabel corrected him.

"Him, too," Stan said.

To face off against a pterodactyl, they would need to be prepared. Dipper and Mabel gathered supplies: maps of the woods, crossbows, flashlights, and other gear. Soos loaded a giant cage into the back of his pickup truck. Then he took some spray paint and christened the truck: PTERODACTYL MOBILE.

"All right!" Soos said, satisfied. "That puh-terodactyl won't know what hit him."

Dipper cringed to hear Soos mispronounce the word. "It's *tero*-dactyl, man."

"Actually, nobody knows how to pronounce it because nobody was alive back in dinosaur days," Soos countered with his special brand of Soos logic.

He got on his back and stuck his head under the truck to affix one of the cage straps to the frame. Suddenly, the truck backfired and started to roll backward. Soos jumped out of the way just in time. The truck stopped moving as quickly as it had started.

"Whoa! Almost ran over my own head there. Heh, heh."

Dipper pulled Mabel aside.

"Mabel, we've gotta talk," he said in a low voice. "This is a really high-stakes mission and I'm a little worried about Soos coming along on this one. I love the guy, but sometimes he messes stuff up."

"What?" Mabel asked. "Well, let him down easy."

Then Soos walked up and wrapped an arm around Dipper. "This is so great! You and me, bro. Best friends. Fighting and potentially high-fiving dinosaurs."

"Uh, Soos, look, I gotta tell you something," Dipper began awkwardly.

"Okay, but before you do, check out these matching shirts I made for us!"

He held up two T-shirts that he had made himself. They read PTERODACTYL BROS. and even had a drawing of Dipper and Soos together.

"Who's this guy here, bro?" Soos asked, pointing to the picture. "You. Totally you, dude. And these rays indicate friendship. So what was it you were going to tell me again?"

Dipper looked nervously at Mabel, who just shrugged. He looked back at Soos, who was already in the driver's seat. He couldn't bear to tell him to stay back now.

"Uh, puh-terodactyl, here we come!" he said with a sigh.

"Yes!" Soos cheered.

Dipper, Mabel, and Stan piled into the truck, and Soos took off. They followed the red thread through the forest to an old abandoned church building. Moss grew up the peeling wooden walls, and the whole building was crooked.

Mabel jumped out of the truck first and followed the red yarn inside as the others followed. Light streamed through the rafters to reveal a skinny old man with a long, white beard.

"Old Man McGucket?" Mabel asked.

"Howdy, friends!" he greeted them as he strummed on his banjo.

"What are you doing out here?" Dipper asked.

"You'll never believe me! I was doing my hourly hootenanny," he replied, and then demonstrated by slapping his hands against his knees, "when this enormous wingy critter stole my musical spoons and flew lickety-split into the abandoned mines down this here hole!"

He pointed at a giant opening in the floor behind him. The red yarn led right down into it. Strange, stinky fumes rose up from the hole. They all peered down.

"Looks kinda hairy down there," Stan said.

"Aw, c'mon, Grunkle Stan," Mabel said. "You can handle it. You punched a pterodactyl in the face, remember?"

"Oh, yeah," Stan said. "Heh, heh. I did do that, didn't I?"

"Guys, we're going in," Mabel said firmly.

"Need someone to tag along and tell weird personal stories?" Old Man McGucket asked.

"No thanks!" Stan said. But Old Man McGucket didn't know the meaning of the word no. Dipper attached a rope to the front of the truck, and dropped the rope down the hole. One by one, they climbed down into the dark abyss.

CHAPTER FOUR

THEY SHINNIED DOWN, down the rope into the creepy darkness. Then . . .

Snap! The rope broke. They fell to the ground below with a thud. Luckily, they hadn't been too high up, and nobody was hurt.

Groaning and brushing off dust, they got on their feet. Dipper led the way with a lantern.

"Whoa," he said, as his eyes adjusted to the dark. There was a whole new world all around them, filled with leafy plants, giant mushrooms, and gnarled redwood tree roots. There were also round, circular pools that looked like Jacuzzis. They steamed, and some shot up sprays of water.

As everyone looked around, amazed, Dipper walked past the geysers and up to one of the plants. "These plants look all Jurassic-y," he remarked.

Soos bent down to sniff a plant with bright pink flowers. "Huh, this little fella smells like battery acid," he said.

Puff! The plant sprayed him with noxious gas.

"Aagh!" Soos cried. Then he chuckled. "Looks like I lost my sense of smell."

Mabel took out the photo of her and Waddles in their silly sunglasses. "Oh, Waddles. We're gonna find you!" she promised.

The huge mouth of an old mining tunnel loomed before them—and the red yarn led right into it. Dipper lit the way as they walked inside. The yellow light of his lantern shone on the rough walls of the cave, and then illuminated the snarling face of a giant *T. rex*!

"Aaaaaaaaaaaah!" everyone screamed.

Then they stopped. The *T. rex* wasn't moving. It seemed frozen. That's when they realized that the beast was imprisoned in a giant mound of amber sap!

Dipper shone the lantern around. Other
dinosaurs were encased in the sap, too.

"They're all trapped inside the tree sap!"
Dipper announced. "*That's* how they survived for
sixty-five million years."

One of the huge sap blocks was empty. They
could make out the outline of a pterodactyl
inside it, and sap was dripping onto the floor of
the mine.

"The summer heat must be melting them
loose," Dipper said.

Stan wandered around, amazed. Where others saw dinosaurs, he saw dollar signs.

"Holy moly! Forget the Corn-icorn—this is the attraction of a lifetime! I could bring people down here and turn this into some sort of theme park. Jurassic Sap Hole!"

"Uh, dudes," Soos said, his voice full of fear.

He pointed to a Velociraptor. One giant, sharp claw of the dinosaur had poked through the melted sap, and was slowly wiggling. . . .

"Guys, maybe we should keep moving," Dipper said.

Stan wasn't listening. "This could be a gold mine!" he said, picturing the attraction in his mind. "Velvety rope-type deal there, ticket booth here. Ha! I shoulda put that pig outside ages ago!"

"Wait, what did you just say?" Mabel asked him.

"Hmm?" Stan said, trying to act innocent.

Mabel pointed at him. "You said the dinosaur flew *into* the house."

Stan stammered. "N-no, that's not what I—"

"You put Waddles outside and you lied to me about it!" Mabel cried. "And now, thanks to you, my pig could be dead."

"Look, he's an animal. He belongs outside," Stan said.

"No. That's it! Grunkle Stan, I am never ever speaking to you again!" Mabel folded her arms across her chest and turned her back to him.

"Mabel, you can't be serious!" Stan said.

"Oh, is someone talking to me right now? Because I can't hear them!" Mabel shot back.

"Kid!" Stan pleaded, but Mabel put her hands over her ears.

"*La la la la la!* I can't hear anyone! No one's talking to me!" she said as she marched away.

"Guys, guys, don't fight! Why can't you be like me and Dipper?" Soos said. He put Dipper into a friendly headlock. Then he picked up the red yarn and started winding it around his meaty hand.

"Everything's gonna be cool. All we gotta do is follow this here yarn! We just keep following and following, and when we reach the end—" Soos looked down at his hand. He had reeled in all the yarn!

"Uh-oh." Soos turned around and looked at a row of mine shafts cut into the wall. "Which cave was it again?"

Dipper threw up his hands in frustration. "Ugh! Soos! You lost the trail!"

"Hey, come on, we'll find our way," Soos said, positive as always. "Trust me!"

He slapped Dipper on the back—hard. The lantern flew out of Dipper's hands and shattered on the floor. The light went out, plunging them all into complete darkness.

"Sorry, dude," Soos said.

"That's it! See, this is why I didn't want to bring you along!" Dipper fumed.

"What do you mean?" Soos asked.

"I mean this is really important to Mabel and you keep screwing everything up!" Dipper yelled. "You ruined our photograph, your dinosaur facts are all wrong, and now you've got us hopelessly lost!"

"But we're Puh-terodactyl Bros," Soos said. "I made T-shirts."

He held up one of the shirts he had made.

"It's pronounced *tero*-dactyl!" Dipper said. "And the shirts are useless! They're gigantic!"

"I have a different body type, dude!" Soos said, angry now.

"Oh, yeah?" Dipper yelled, and he and Soos started shouting at each other. Then Mabel and Stan started to argue.

"Hey!" Old Man McGucket's voice quieted everyone down. "Cheer up, fellers! I fixed yer lantern!"

He held up the lantern—and the light illuminated a huge pterodactyl standing right behind him!

CHAPTER FIVE

"**A**AAAAAAAAAAAAAAAAAH!"
screamed Stan, Mabel, Dipper, and Soos.

"*Aaaaaaaaaaaaaaaah!*" screamed Old Man
McGucket, who still had no idea that there was
a huge pterodactyl behind him. Then he laughed.
"What are we doing?"

Seeing the terrified expressions in front of him, he slowly turned around and saw the pterodactyl. The beast looked back at him with an unnerving reptilian stare.

"Nobody make any sudden movements or noises," he warned softly. Then he jumped up and yelled, "Yee-hawww! We found a pterodactyl!"

The pterodactyl shrieked, revealing a mouth full of razor-sharp teeth. Then it charged. Screaming, everybody ran into the nearest mine shaft.

The pterodactyl's head got stuck, buying them time. They ran through the shaft and emerged into an enormous cavern. The cart tracks traveled across a huge chasm to the other side.

"Aaaaiiieeeeeeee!" The pterodactyl's shriek rang out behind them. They quickly hid behind some stalagmites sticking up from the ground.

"Guys, we gotta think of a plan!" Dipper said.

"Okay, okay," Stan said. "Howsabout Mabel knits Soos a pig costume . . ."

"I like it!" Soos said.

"... and we use Soos as a human sacrifice," Stan finished.

"I like it!" Soos said.

"Whaddya say, Mabel?" Stan asked her, but Mabel just looked away.

"Aw, come on, you can't stop talking to me forever!" Stan pleaded.

"Yeah, Mabel, we have to work together here," Dipper said.

Soos glared at him. "Oh, so you wanna work with Mabel, but not your buddy Soos?" he asked.

They all started arguing again.

"Oink! Oink!"

The sound echoed across the cavern. Mabel's eyes got wide.

"Wait! Did you hear that?" she asked. Peeking out from behind the rock, she saw Waddles. The pterodactyl had made a huge nest on an isolated rock tower in the middle of the

cavern, high above the chasm. Inside the nest was one huge white egg—and one small pink pig.

"Waddles!" Mabel cried.

She jumped up and ran onto the cart track, following it over the safety of the ledge and onto the stretch of rickety track that spanned the deep, wide chasm.

"Stop, kid!" Stan yelled, and everyone jumped up to chase her. But Mabel was halfway to the nest by now.

"Are you nuts?" Stan called out to her.

Mabel stopped. "Oh, is someone speaking? Because I can't hear anything!"

"Oh, no! She's gone deaf with fear!" wailed Old Man McGucket (who just didn't get it).

Mabel turned and kept running until she reached the nest. "Oh, my Waddles! I'll never lose you again!" she promised, hugging him to her.

Dipper, Soos, Stan, and Old Man McGucket caught up to her.

"Uh . . . M-Mabel?" Dipper stammered nervously. His sister was too caught up in Waddles to notice what else was in the nest. Namely, the skeletons of old miners.

"Mabel, great, you got him," Dipper said. "Now we gotta get outta here!"

"Okay," Mabel said. "Let me just get this thing on." She took the Huggy Wuvvy Tummy Bundle out of her backpack and put it on Waddles.

"*Aaaaaaiiiieeeeee!*"

The pterodactyl swooped in, shrieking and flying over the nest. Terrified, Waddles wiggled out of Mabel's grasp and ran out of the nest and onto the cart track. He jumped on top of Stan.

"Get off me, you dumb pig!" Stan yelled, grabbing Waddles.

The pterodactyl swooped down again, and everyone in the nest ducked. The dinosaur stomped on the track, breaking it. Stan and Waddles plummeted into the chasm.

They fell down, down, and then bounced off the top of a giant, spongy mushroom. A second mushroom cushioned their fall, and then they landed with a splash in a puddle of muck. Waddles rolled around in it happily.

"Aaaaaaaiiiieeeeee!"

The pterodactyl lunged, attacking them feet-first. It grabbed Stan's red fez in its claws and then flew up, dropping the hat into the nest. Mabel picked it up.

"We've got to save them!" Mabel cried.

Dipper thought quickly. Old Man McGucket could actually be pretty innovative at times.

"McGucket! Do you have any inventions on you that can distract it?" he asked.

"Do I ever!" the old man replied with a huge grin. He took off his hat and began rooting around inside it. "Nope!"

Then they heard the sound of an egg cracking. They slowly turned to see the huge white egg crack open—and the face of a baby pterodactyl peeked out. The ten-foot-tall infant crawled out of the egg and stared at them blankly.

"Awww!" Mabel said.

Old Man McGucket grinned. "Well, welcome to the world, little—"

Gulp! The baby pterodactyl opened its mouth and swallowed McGucket in one bite.

Dipper, Mabel, and Soos screamed.

Down below, Stan and Waddles took refuge under a big mushroom as the mother pterodactyl flew overhead.

"The dumb thing must be hungry," Stan said. "I guess it's you or me, pig."

With his foot, he slowly pushed Waddles out into the open. The pig turned and stared at him.

"What are ya looking at?" Stan growled.

Waddles just kept staring at him.

"Come on! Don't gimme that look. What am I supposed to do? Let it eat *me*?" Stan asked.

Waddles stared at him some more.

"Yeah, I get it!" Stan fumed. "You're trying to guilt me, but it ain't working. Who cares if you're the kid's favorite thing in the world? I can live without Mabel talking to me all the time . . .

telling me her jokes . . . making me laugh."

He felt sadder and sadder as he thought about it. He looked at Waddles, then at the face of Mabel on Waddles's sweater.

"Oh, dang it!" he said with a sigh. He ran out from under the mushroom and grabbed Waddles. Then he strapped the pig to his back with the Huggy Wuvvy Tummy Bundle.

"Aaaaiiiiieeeeeee!"

The pterodactyl spotted him. It charged from above. Stan stood firm, his fists clenched.

"Well, this is just about the dumbest thing I've ever done," he muttered to himself. He took a deep breath, and then yelled as loud as he could at the approaching dinosaur.

"You want this pig? Then come at me, you flying devil!"

CHAPTER SIX

UP IN THE NEST, Dipper, Mabel, and Soos stared in horror at the baby pterodactyl.

"Dude, did he really just eat that prospector guy?" Soos asked.

Then the baby burped, and Old Man McGucket's head popped out of its beak.

"I'm okay!" he said with a wave, and then the pterodactyl baby gulped him down again.

"What do we do?" Dipper wailed.

"We have to get in a line," Soos said.

"What?" Mabel asked.

"I read it somewhere," Soos explained. "A puh-terodactyl's eyes are so far apart, that if you stand right in front of it, it can't see you."

Dipper was doubtful. "Soos, you've been wrong about stuff all day! How can we—"

"Dude, I know I've messed up a lot," Soos interrupted him. "I can be sorta clumsy and it's not always as lovable as I think but please, as my friend, just trust me on this one."

The baby pterodactyl was munching on Old Man McGucket's hat. Dipper knew when it finished with that, it would come after them. He nodded at Soos.

"Behind me, dudes!" Soos said bravely.

Dipper and Mabel got in a straight line behind Soos. They slowly made their way behind the baby beast, moving backward.

The pterodactyl suddenly lifted its head, and they froze. It turned, facing them directly, but it didn't seem to see them—just as Soos had said.

"It's working!" Mabel whispered.

Slowly, they backed out of the nest onto the tracks that bridged the chasm. Confused, the baby pterodactyl waddled backward and turned to the nest, nibbling at the dead miners' bones.

Dipper, Mabel, and Soos reached the other side and sat behind the stalagmites, relieved.

"Soos! You did it!" Dipper cheered.

"Aaaaaiiiiieeeeeeeeee!"

The terrifying screech of the mother pterodactyl rang through the cavern. Looking up, they saw her flying around, careening wildly and spinning in circles.

She got closer, and that's when they saw him—Stan, riding the pterodactyl like a cowboy astride a bucking bronco. He had Waddles strapped to him, and he was furiously punching the beast in the face!

Dipper, Soos, and Mabel watched, amazed. Confused, the pterodactyl crashed into the ledge. Stan jumped off before the beast plummeted to the bottom of the chasm. Dipper, Soos, and Mabel rushed toward him, cheering.

Stan pulled Waddles out of the Huggy Wuvvy Tummy Bundle and handed him to Mabel.

"Here's your pig, kiddo," Stan said.

Mabel hugged Waddles tightly. "Waddles!" she

cried happily. Then she looked at her great-uncle in amazement.

"You saved him for me," she told Stan.

Stan shrugged. "Yeah, well—*look out!*"

The pterodactyl's huge head appeared over the ridge. They screamed and ran back through the mining tunnel as the angry dinosaur crawled after them, its huge beak snapping.

When they exited the tunnel, the pterodactyl took to the air. Screaming and running as fast as they could, they raced past the dinosaurs encased in sap. They reached the mine shaft and looked up—to see the broken rope swinging above them, just out of reach. There was no way out!

Then Dipper noticed something—one of the steaming geysers was positioned directly under the church. It shot up a powerful blast of water.

"Quick! It can shoot us back up!" Dipper said.

They all climbed into the geyser, waiting for

the next burst
to send them
shooting to
safety. The
pterodactyl
swooped
down at them
and opened its
beak wide.

"Bros before dinoooooooos!" Soos yelled, and gave the walls of the geyser a mighty smack, kick-starting it. A jet of water blasted them straight up.

"*Whoooooooaaaaaaaaaaaa!*" they screamed as the geyser rocketed them back up into the church. They blasted through the rickety wood roof and came back down on a pile of debris.

Panting and exhausted, they quickly left the old church as the roof collapsed, filling up the huge hole leading to the dinosaur world.

"I can't believe you did all that for Waddles," Mabel told Stan.

"Well, I can't have my favorite great-niece not talking to me. And if I gotta leap onto a pterodactyl and punch it in the face, then that's what I gotta do," Stan said, leaning against a tree.

"That's kind of sappy," Mabel said.

"Well, that's how I feel," Stan told her.

Mabel pointed. "No, I mean . . ."

Sap was oozing from the tree, and now it covered Stan's hand. Grinning, he stuck his hand on Mabel's face.

"Gotcha!" Then he tried to take his hand off—but they were stuck!

Dipper and Soos helped them get unstuck, and soon a sticky Stan, Mabel, and Waddles were snoozing in the backseat as Soos drove them all home. Dipper took off his vest.

"Check it out. That thing destroyed my vest," he said. Then something fell into his hand. "Look!"

He held up a large gray tooth.

"A real dinosaur tooth! Dude, that's awesome," Soos said.

"Not as awesome as you saving us back there," Dipper said. He held up his fist for a pound. "Pterodactyl Bros?"

Soos fist-bumped him. "Pterodactyl Bros. Hey, I pronounced it right that time!"

Dipper looked into the rearview mirror at the old church as it faded into the distance. "Think we need to worry about the rest of those dinosaurs?"

"I doubt it," Soos said.

Back in the old church, something pushed through the debris in the hole leading to the dinosaur world. The board creaked, revealing . . .

. . . Old Man McGucket, holding his spoons.

"I ate my way through a dinosaur!"